POPCORN

Alex Moran
Illustrated by Betsy Everitt

Green Light Readers
Harcourt Brace & Company
San Diego   New York   London

Requests for permission to make copies of any part of the work should be mailed to:
Permissions Department, Harcourt Brace & Company, 6277 Sea Harbor Drive,
Orlando, Florida 32887-6777.

First Green Light Readers edition 1999
Green Light Readers is a trademark of Harcourt Brace & Company.

The Library of Congress has cataloged the original paperback edition as follows:
Moran, Alex.
Popcorn/Alex Moran; illustrated by Betsy Everitt.
p.   cm.
"Green Light Readers."
Summary: Illustrations and rhythmic, rhyming text show what happens
when popping popcorn gets out of hand.
[1. Popcorn—Fiction. 2. Stories in rhyme.] I. Everitt, Betsy, ill. II. Title.
PZ8.3.M795Po 1999
[E]—dc21   98-15566
ISBN 0-15-201998-7 (pb)

ISBN 0-15-202375-5

B D F G E C (pb)

A C E F D B

Printed in Mexico

Popcorn. Popcorn.

Put it in a pot.

Popcorn. Popcorn.

Get the pot hot.

Popcorn. Popcorn.
Put in lots more.

Popcorn. Popcorn.
One, two, three, four.

Popcorn. Popcorn.
Pop! Pop! Pop!

Popcorn. Popcorn.
Stop! Stop! Stop!

Popcorn. Popcorn.
What is the plan?

Popcorn. Popcorn.
Catch it if you can!

Popcorn. Popcorn.
It's going out the door.

Popcorn. Popcorn.
Stop! No more!

Popcorn. Popcorn.
Get it while it's hot.

We are happy.
We like it a lot!

Meet the Illustrator

Betsy Everitt likes to go to the movies and get a big bucket of popcorn. She and her family like to make popcorn at home, too.

Betsy Everitt chose animals with nice shapes and used lots of bright colors for this story. She put the colors and shapes together to create feelings. How do you feel when you look at her pictures?

BETSY EVERITT